THE SEA D

DRAGON

Zoe the
Beach Dragon

Maddy Mara

📖 SCHOLASTIC

DRAGON GIRLS

Zoe the Beach Dragon

by Maddy Mara

Scholastic Inc.

ISBN 978-1-338-87549-2

10 9 8 7 6 5 4 3 2 1   23 24 25 26 27

Printed in the U.S.A. 40

First printing 2023

Book design by Cassy Price

1

Zoe sat on her yellow surfboard, floating on the water. She scanned the horizon. Were there any good waves coming?

Zoe had been going surfing with her dad and big sister ever since she was really small. Riding a surfboard felt almost as natural as walking. She loved being out in the glittering sea, waves breaking around her. It was amazing how all Zoe's worries disappeared when she was on her board. Nothing beat the feeling of riding a wave all the way to shore! Zoe could do it all day.

That's why Zoe's mom had suggested sleepaway aquatics camp this summer. Zoe had jumped at the idea! So far, camp had been as good as she'd hoped. In fact, it had been way better. For one thing, she got to surf every day. For another, there were so many great kids to get to know. Zoe got along with most people. But she had formed a special bond with her cabinmates, Grace and Sofia.

All these things combined to make camp fantastic. But there was something else. Something that made it ... magical. Zoe, Sofia, and Grace had found out that they were able to travel to another realm. It was called the Magic Forest. When they were there, they became dragons. Not just ordinary dragons, either. Sea Dragons, to be exact!

The three new friends had already had one adventure in the Magic Forest. They had helped the Tree Queen, who was the ruler of the Magic Forest, by rescuing a missing dolphin. Acing the quest had felt incredible, and the Tree Queen told them she would need their help again. Zoe could hardly wait to return. She was glad that she had surfing to keep her mind busy until that happened!

Every day at camp, Zoe went with the other surfing kids to the local surf beach. Their coach, Stef, surfed alongside them, giving them tips to improve their skills. Zoe had already learned so much.

Zoe did not see her new friends during the day, because Grace was a swimmer and Sofia a diver. This meant they each had different activities in other locations. But that was fine. It was fun talking about their days when they caught up every afternoon.

Today, Zoe had already been in the water for

an hour. But it felt like only a few minutes.

Up ahead, she spotted a wave beginning to swell. Zoe started to paddle, getting herself into a good position as she waited for the wave to build. When Zoe was surfing, everything else dropped away. She thought about just two things: the board beneath her, and the move-ment of the water around her.

"Get ready, Zoe!" called Stef from nearby. "That wave is going to be huge!"

It was time. Zoe sprang up onto her board. She landed perfectly, crouching low, her left foot forward. She started coasting along the lifting wave. Foamy white droplets splashed down over her as the wave began to curve. Zoe could hear the swell of the ocean all around her, the waves crashing on the shore. But she could hear something else, too.

Magic Forest, Magic Forest, come explore...

Excitement bubbled in Zoe—and it wasn't about the perfect wave she was riding. She'd heard that song before. It had been when she traveled to the Magic Forest last time! Was she about to go back? Oh, she hoped so!

The wave Zoe was riding stretched on and on. She felt like she was surfing through a beautiful blue tunnel. Zoe heard the song again. It blended with the sound of the sea itself.

Magic Forest, Magic Forest, come explore.

Zoe stretched out a hand and trailed it along the wave. Her silver bracelet with its fan-shaped shell glinted on her wrist. The Tree Queen had given one each to Zoe, Grace, and

Sofia. Usually the shells were white. But right now, Zoe's glowed pale aqua.

Zoe's heart thumped. She was sure of it. She was about to be sent on her second magical quest! She had a feeling that this quest would be even harder than the first. But that probably meant it would be even more exciting. Then she heard the final line in the song.

Magic Forest, Magic Forest, hear my roar!

Zoe grinned. She loved roaring when she was a dragon. It was such a powerful, freeing feeling. She couldn't wait to do it again.

Finally, the wave crashed, pulling Zoe off her board. Zoe went with the flow and closed her eyes. She hoped that when she opened them again, she would be in a very different place!

Zoe rose to the surface of the water and burst through. Air filled her lungs and the sun warmed her face. She hadn't opened her eyes yet. Had she been transported into the Magic Forest? She hardly dared to look! The water felt softer and warmer. And the waves sounded different somehow. Rather than crashing, they made a magical tinkly sound. It reminded Zoe of wind chimes, blown by a summer breeze.

Zoe opened her eyes. Looking around, she saw she was still at a surf beach. But it was not the same one she'd just left. All the other surfers in her group had disappeared. The people who had been sitting on the beach were gone, too. Before, there had been beach shacks lining the shore. Now the shacks had been replaced with tall trees.

A shiver of excitement passed through Zoe. *The Magic Forest!*

Treading water, Zoe glanced down at herself. She grinned at what she saw. Yes! She was back in her dragon form! Her body was covered with sandy-yellow scales, tipped with blue. She had a long, swishy tail that made treading water as easy as breathing. She also had a fabulous pair of wings. Zoe gave them a huge flap and rose smoothly out of the water.

She zoomed up, sending shimmering droplets of water in every direction. Surfing would always be Zoe's first love. But flying was a very, very close second.

"Flying is like surfing in the air, isn't it?" said a friendly little voice.

Zoe looked down. Swimming in the sea below her was the tiniest penguin Zoe had ever seen. It looked up at Zoe with big blue eyes.

"Hello there. Yes, that's exactly what it's like!"

agreed Zoe, swooping around and coming back to hover near the tiny penguin. A thought crossed her mind. "But how do you know that? I know that penguins can surf. But they can't fly, can they?"

Instead of answering, the penguin flapped its stubby little wings furiously. To Zoe's great surprise, the penguin flew up into the air beside her. Even more surprising was how the tiny creature looked. Zoe had never seen a purple-and-white penguin before!

"I'm a pixie penguin," explained the bird. "My name's Splashi."

"Hi, Splashi! I'm Zoe," Zoe said. "I'm a Sea Dragon."

Splashi did a twirl. She had a funny way of flying. Her whole body seemed to waddle. But Zoe was careful not to laugh. She didn't want to hurt the little bird's feelings.

"Oh, I know that!" said Splashi. "I've been waiting for you to arrive. The Tree Queen wants me to bring you to her as quickly as possible. She really needs help from you and your friends."

"Let's go, then!" Zoe said.

Surfing had taught Zoe to act quickly. And she wanted to leap into this adventure as soon as possible.

Together, Splashi and Zoe flew over the sparkling sea toward the huge trees of the Magic Forest. A strong wind blew in from the shore. It almost felt as if it was trying to stop them from getting to the Magic Forest.

"The wind is part of the Fire Queen's magic," Splashi explained. "She was furious when you and the other Sea Dragons rescued the first

Sea Keeper. She is determined to stop you from rescuing the others."

Zoe flapped her wings harder than ever. The Fire Queen could make the strongest winds she wanted. There was no way a bit of hot air was going to stop the Sea Dragons!

Splashi led the way high above the beach and into the forest. Zoe had been here only once before. Yet the Magic Forest already felt familiar to her. Zoe breathed in the rich scent of tropical fruit and flowers. The sounds of birds filled the air. Their songs were beautiful, but Zoe sensed a note of danger in the bird-calls, too.

Splashi flew closer. "We need to be care-ful in here. The Fire Queen has been waiting for your return. Her Fire Sparks are lurking everywhere."

Zoe shuddered, remembering the nasty sparks from her last visit. Zoe loved every-thing about nature. She even loved the parts that weren't cute or friendly. She never killed spiders. She knew lots about grizzly bears. And she thought the worms in their garden at home were cool.

But the Fire Sparks were very hard to like! They could give you a nasty sting. Their bright glow made it hard to see. Worst of all, when the sparks swooshed around your head, you ended up feeling very confused and forgetful. It was all part of their evil magic.

But I won't let them stop me, Zoe decided.

The strong wind seemed to follow Zoe and Splashi as they flew deeper into the forest. It whipped between the trees, making the leaves rustle wildly. Twirls of dirt blew up from the forest floor, filling Zoe's eyes with grit. She blinked away the dust and continued, weaving between the tall trees. The farther into the forest Zoe and Splashi went, the darker it became. The birdsong dropped away, and soon all that could be heard was the wind.

Zoe got the strange feeling that the forest creatures were hiding.

Out of the corner of her eye, Zoe saw a pin-prick of light hovering in the leaves. Then she saw another. And another! Soon the trees all around were full of bright lights.

"Fire Sparks!" Splashi warned. "Let's speed up!"

Zoe flapped her powerful wings as the Fire Sparks left their shadowy hiding places. They darted after her. Zoe frowned as she ducked and swooped. Was she imagining it, or were they larger than the last time?

The air filled with the sound of angry buzz-ing. The Fire Sparks shot forward, trying to sting Zoe's wings and poor little Splashi's

colorful body. Zoe swished the sparks away as best she could and kept going. They just needed to make it as far as the Tree Queen's glade. Zoe knew it must be close.

At least, she thought it was close. Her head was starting to feel foggy and unclear.

"They're trying to muddle you," Splashi whispered. "Whatever you do, just keep following me."

But just then, a swarm of Fire Sparks surrounded Splashi. The penguin was thrown back and forth like a boat in stormy seas.

Zoe felt a fury grow inside her. Most of the time she was pretty relaxed. But one thing she couldn't stand? Bullies.

"Stop that NOW!" Zoe roared at the Fire Sparks.

The roar burst from her and sent Fire Sparks scattering. They spun off away between the trees. Zoe watched to see if any of them dared to come back.

But none of the sparks returned. For now, at least, they were safe.

Splashi flew up and nuzzled Zoe under her

chin. "Thanks, Zoe," said the little penguin. "I hope I can return the favor before this adventure is over. And look, we're here."

Between the trees Zoe saw a pulsing light, warm and inviting. It was the shimmering force field of the Tree Queen's glade!

3

Even though they were deep in the forest, the wind still whipped through the trees. Instead of fighting it, Zoe used the gusts to lift her closer to the glade's force field. It was like surfing in midair! Hovering, Zoe turned to the little penguin.

"Thank you for leading me here," she said. "Will we meet again?"

Splashi zoomed closer and gave Zoe a peck on the cheek. "Of course we will! You have a big quest ahead of you. I will be there the moment you need me."

The little creature did a final loop and then flew off into the forest in her funny, waddly way.

Another gust of wind rushed through. Zoe rode the wind all the way around the outside of the glade. She could see the faint outline of a huge tree through the shimmery air.

The Tree Queen, Zoe thought.

Then she saw two other shapes flying inside.

One was coral-colored. The other was aqua.

Zoe smiled. Grace and Sofia were already here!

Tipping her wings, Zoe skimmed the force field.

Then, as if she was ducking through a wave, she pushed through the warm fuzzy air and into the glade. Instantly, the scent of fruit and flowers became stronger. Like the last time Zoe had visited, the glade's air was warm and calm, and the birdsong more melodious.

An excited cry went up. "Zoe is here!"

A moment later, Zoe was caught up in a mid-air wing-hug.

"We're Sea Dragons again!" whooped Grace, the aqua-colored dragon.

"And we're about to start another quest!"

added Sofia, the coral-colored dragon. "Look! The Tree Queen is appearing."

The huge tree at the center of the glade had begun to sway. Its branches were laden with fruits that looked like peaches. But as the tree moved, the scent of strawberries filled the air. Zoe smiled. The Magic Forest was truly a remarkable place. Soon, the tree's trunk became a regal-looking woman wearing a mossy-green gown.

The Tree Queen smiled kindly at the group. "My dear Sea Dragons! Thank you for returning to the Magic Forest so quickly," she said in her warm voice.

Zoe, Sofia, and Grace moved closer until they hovered in the air before the queen.

"I am so glad to see you three again," the queen continued. "As you know, the Fire Queen captured the three Sea Keepers. You have already rescued the dolphin leader, and we are very grateful."

Zoe and her friends exchanged a proud look. On their last trip to the Magic Forest, they had met the Diamond Dolphins of Dolphin Cove. They had also had tea with some Shiver Sharks, who turned out to be more scared than scary. And they had roared away the Fire Sparks. It had been an amazing adventure. What lay ahead of them this time?

"But there are still two Sea Keepers missing," continued the Tree Queen, her leaves rustling. "This time, I'd like you to find the second Sea Keeper. She is the turtle leader."

"We'll find the turtle," Sofia said firmly.

Zoe smiled at her friend. She had not known Sofia very long, but she already knew that when Sofia said she'd do something, she really meant it.

"I know you will do your very best," the Tree Queen said. Then her broad smile faded just a little. "But this quest will be harder than the last, I am afraid. Time is running out. Literally! The Sea Keepers meet in the Undersea Garden every full moon. As I have explained, once a year on the full moon, they must wind up the Water Watch. And that moment is fast approaching."

Zoe opened her mouth to ask a question. But the Tree Queen already seemed to know what she was going to ask!

"The Water Watch is an ancient object," she

explained. "It keeps the tides flowing as they should. And it makes sure that the seas are at the right level."

Zoe gave her sandy-colored tail a swish. "What happens if the Water Watch doesn't get wound on time?" she asked.

The Tree Queen frowned. "I am afraid chaos will strike our seas, and the Fire Queen will..." She trailed off.

"What would she do?" Sofia asked, her voice a whisper.

"We do not know for certain," said the Tree Queen, "but as I said last time you were here, we strongly suspect that the Fire Queen is planning to drain the seas."

The three Sea Dragons were silent. Zoe had loved the ocean her entire life. She adored surfing it, of course. But that was only one part of it. She loved how the water changed constantly throughout the day—and from one day to the next. She loved the salty smell and feel of it. And there were so many amazing creatures that lived in the sea.

How could anyone hate something so wonderful? As for the idea of draining it . . . that was unthinkable!

"It is terrible, I know," said the Tree Queen softly. "The Fire Queen thinks of water as her enemy. By getting rid of the seas, I suspect she plans to gain more power."

"Well, we won't let her do that," Zoe said, turning to her friends. "Will we?"

"No way," Sofia said.

"Absolutely not!" Grace agreed. She flapped her wings so hard that the grass down on the ground bent almost flat.

The Tree Queen's smile returned. "Don't forget that you have your shell bracelets. They will help guide you when you need it."

"Should we start at Dolphin Cove again?" Grace asked.

The Tree Queen swayed back and forth. Zoe could sense that she was about to turn back into a tree. "Not this time," she said, her voice growing softer and leafier by the second. "Begin at Turtle Surf Beach. Ask the hatchlings if they saw anything. Good luck, Sea Dragons! And don't forget: Your power is even greater when you work together."

"Excuse me, but what hatchlings?" Zoe asked quickly. She wanted just a little more information before they set out on this next quest.

But there was no reply. The queen was once again a tree.

4

Zoe felt a gentle tug. The shell on her bracelet was glowing.

"Try holding it up to your ear," Grace advised.

Zoe did so, and heard the sound of distant waves crashing on the sand. Then a voice mingled with the waves.

"I will guide you to Turtle Surf Beach."

Zoe turned to her friends, who were hovering in the air beside her. "My shell is going to show us the way."

"Then what are we waiting for?" Sofia flapped her wings in excitement. "Let's go!"

Together, the Sea Dragons flew back through the shimmering force field and into the forest. The cool air of the Magic Forest brushed past the three friends as they made their way through the trees, turning this way and that to fit through the narrow gaps.

Zoe led the way, following the gentle tugs on her paw from the bracelet.

"Have you spotted any Fire Sparks?" she asked Sofia and Grace.

"Not yet." Sofia shook her head.

"I haven't, either," Grace said. "But somehow I get the feeling they're not far away."

Zoe nodded. "Same. But don't worry. If those sparks try anything, we'll be ready for them!"

Zoe roared loudly, and her friends joined in. The powerful sound echoed through the trees. Zoe grinned. That would show any lurking Fire Sparks that the Sea Dragons were not afraid!

Before long, the shell had guided the group out of the forest and all the way to a beach.

Instantly, Zoe recognized it. "This is where I arrived!"

"Hey, what are those things?" Sofia pointed a talon to a nearby sand dune.

Halfway up crawled a group of very small creatures. They had shiny blue shells and long necks. Their little legs scrabbled furiously in the sand.

"Wow! Baby turtles!" Zoe exclaimed. "They must be the hatchlings the Tree Queen mentioned."

"Why are they trying to climb that sand dune?" Grace wondered. "Shouldn't they be heading for the water?"

"You're right," said Zoe. "They must be confused. Let's go help them."

Zoe whooshed across the sand, her friends close behind. As they came close to the turtles, Zoe flew lower and slowed down.

"You're going the wrong way!" she called to the baby turtles.

She tried to speak as softly as she could. But even a dragon's whisper is loud! The baby turtles squeaked in surprise. Then, to Zoe's dismay, the little creatures began to roll backward down the sand dune.

"Oh, the poor darlings!" Grace cooed.

Zoe could tell Grace was trying not to laugh. The tiny, tumbling turtles looked very funny.

The Sea Dragons flew down to the bottom of the sand dune—just as the turtles landed there in a heap. The hatchlings lay at the base of the dune on their backs, their legs wiggling in the air.

"They're stuck," Zoe said, also trying not to laugh. "Come on, let's help them."

Zoe, Sofia, and Grace flew from turtle to turtle, gently scooping up each baby and placing it the right way up on the sand.

"There you go! Now, can we ask you guys some questions?" Grace asked the hatchlings.

"Sure you can, in a minute!" called one little turtle with a very shiny blue shell. "But first, can you take us up to the top of the dune so we can roll down again?"

"Yes! Please do!" called all the other hatchlings, dancing on their feet with excitement.

"I'm glad that was fun. But you should be swimming in the sea, not playing in the sand dunes!" Zoe said, struggling not to giggle. "Anyway, aren't you hungry?"

"We are very hungry," said one of the turtles. "But we do NOT want to go in the sea!"

"Why?" Zoe was surprised. She knew that the first thing sea turtles usually did after hatching was head for the water. They were much safer there. And they could look for food in the sea.

But these baby turtles were all huddled together, and suddenly looked scared.

"It's because of the Wrong Way Wave," whispered the littlest hatchling. "We don't want it to catch us and pull us too far out!"

Zoe and her friends looked at one another. Wrong Way Wave? What could that possibly mean?

There was a sudden whoosh of air above them. The turtles whimpered and quickly pulled their heads and legs into their shells.

The Sea Dragons looked up and saw a huge gull swooping toward them. It was much bigger than the gulls Zoe was used to at home. Plus, it had fierce-looking eyes, like an eagle. Right now, those eyes were fixed on the hatchlings! Zoe stiffened.

"Don't you dare try to scare these little turtles," she warned the gull. "Or worse, eat them!"

"I wasn't planning on it," the gull squawked. "Turtles are far too salty for my liking. I was coming to give you some important information. But maybe you don't want it?"

"Sorry!" Zoe said quickly. "I didn't mean to be rude. What information do you have?"

The gull flew lower, until it hovered at the same level as the Sea Dragons.

"Those turtle kids are right about the Wrong

Way Wave," the gull muttered from the side of his beak. "I saw it with my own eagle eyes."

Zoe felt a shiver pass through her. She wasn't sure what a Wrong Way Wave might be, but it did not sound good!

"I was flying over the beach this time yesterday," continued the gull, "and a huge wave lifted up near the shore. It was a strange-looking thing. Instead of white foam at the edge, it was topped with ... fire."

Zoe and her friends exchanged a surprised look. *A wave topped with fire?* That was very odd indeed. The Fire Queen just *had* to be responsible!

The gull looked at the Sea Dragons, his big

eyes wide. "And instead of breaking on the shore, like a normal wave, it picked up a turtle from the beach and then rolled back into the ocean."

For a moment, Zoe almost forgot to flap her wings. "You saw this weird wave pick up a turtle?" she repeated, her heart pounding.

"Yep," replied the gull. "It was a big turtle, too. Not like these baby ones."

"That was probably the turtle Sea Keeper!" Sofia gasped.

"Exactly what I was thinking," Grace agreed. "But what should we do? The ocean is huge. That wave could have taken the turtle anywhere."

Zoe gazed out at the sparkling water.

Sofia looked at her curiously. "What are you doing?"

"I'm reading the sea," Zoe explained. "If the Wrong Way Wave was here at this time yesterday, it will probably come again soon. And you know what we're going to do when it comes, right?"

Grace and Sofia looked at Zoe. They both looked doubtful.

"Um ... you're not going to *surf* it, are you?" Grace asked.

"Of course I am!" Zoe cried. "And not just me. You are, too!"

The giant gull laughed. "Good luck with that, Sea Dragons. That wave is very unusual. It's not going to be easy to surf."

"We'll be fine," Zoe said quickly. She didn't want the gull to scare her friends. "Thanks so much for your help."

"No problem!" the gull squawked.

He flapped his huge wings and flew away.

"Do you *really* think we'll be fine?" Sofia asked. "Grace and I have never surfed normal waves before—let alone magical ones going the wrong way!"

"And what about the baby turtles?" Grace added. "We can't just leave them here."

Zoe scanned the ocean again. It was mostly calm. But she could see something odd. Close to the shore, the water was beginning to rise. Big waves usually formed far out at sea, not near the shoreline. Even stranger, this wave had a fiery glow to it.

It has to be the Wrong Way Wave! Zoe

thought. She knew she had to act fast. Waves waited for no one!

Quickly, Zoe flew back to the baby turtles. "If you thought rolling down a sand dune was fun, wait until you try flying!" she said. "Climb onto my back."

Squealing with excitement, the hatchlings began scrabbling up onto Zoe's back. It was not easy for the little creatures with their stumpy legs. Luckily, Grace and Sofia were there to help nudge them up.

Once they were all safely on board, Zoe flew high into the air once more. "Hold on tight!" she warned the turtles, who yelled joyfully.

"You look like a ride at a fairground!" Grace laughed, flying alongside Zoe.

"You really do!" Sofia agreed, coming up on the other side.

"I feel like one!" Zoe said. "And you have no idea how ticklish it is to have a bunch of baby turtles on your back."

Luckily, it was only a short flight from the sand dune to the edge of the sea. As Zoe approached the shore, she flew low, just skimming the water.

Zoe flew to a safe part of the shore. It was far from the strange wave that was starting to form.

"Jump off now!" she instructed the turtles.

At first the turtles did not want to jump into the sea. But then one baby slid into the water.

"It's great in here!" it called to the others. "Even better than the sand!"

With that, all the hatchlings leapt from Zoe's back and into the water. Soon they were all splashing about happily.

"Come and swim with us, Sea Dragons!" they called.

"Another time!" Zoe promised. Swimming with baby turtles would be fun. But Zoe also knew there was no time for fun right now. The swelling she'd spotted was rapidly turning into a wave. It was not curving toward the shore like a normal wave. Instead, it was facing the deep water and the horizon—the wrong way!

And, just as the gull had said, the wave was crested with fire. It was a very strange sight. A beautiful blue wave tipped with bright red flames instead of white foam!

Zoe took a deep breath. It was not going to be easy to ride this thing. But that made it more exciting.

"Follow me," Zoe called to her friends. "We can do this, I know it. The main thing is to stay just ahead of where the wave is breaking."

Zoe led the way over to the remarkable wave. Fiery drops cascaded down from its edge, sizzling as they hit the water. Expertly, Zoe bodysurfed within the curl, so that she was just resting on the water. Grace and Sofia did the same, right behind her.

"You guys are natural bodysurfers!" Zoe called. "Now, stay calm, and use your wings for balance!"

Zoe had surfed some big waves in her time. But she had never surfed a wave like this. Most waves moved at a steady pace. But this one was fast one minute, then slow the next. Even stranger, the wave seemed to be twitching. It twisted back and forth, stopping and starting.

"I'm not sure how much longer I—" Sofia was cut short.

The wave had suddenly shot high into the air! Then the massive wall of water began to shake and twist back and forth. It was like a wild horse trying to buck off the Sea Dragons! Fiery sparks rained down around them, hissing as the water evaporated.

Then the wave crashed, dunking Zoe and her friends into the sea. Zoe had wiped out many times. It was a normal part of surfing. But this was different. Once they were deep underwater, the wave didn't release them like a normal wave would. Instead, it gripped on to them, spinning them around.

Over and over the three Sea Dragons tumbled, like socks in a washing machine. Even worse, the fiery sparks from the crest of the wave were swirling in the water, too.

Zoe knew that whenever the Fire Sparks were nearby, she started to feel confused. This time was worse than ever.

She tried to look through the churning water.

Which way was up? Then she started to wonder why they had been surfing in the first place. Her thoughts swirled. Zoe closed her eyes, trying to get her mind in order.

Suddenly, she heard a familiar voice in her ear. "Hold paws with your friends," said the voice. "That will steady you all."

Splash!? Zoe opened her eyes.

Sure enough, swishing along beside her was the little pixie penguin. Just seeing her bright purple wings made Zoe feel better. It also made her more determined.

Through the churning water, Zoe saw something coral-colored. Sofia! Reaching out, she grabbed hold of Sofia's paw. Instantly, her head felt a bit clearer.

Where was Grace? Ah, there she was! Zoe took hold of Grace's paw, and Sofia took hold of Grace's other one. Now they had formed a circle.

Zoe felt power surge through her. The swirling water steadied for a moment. But Zoe sensed that their ordeal was not over. A moment later, the water rose once more, carrying them upward. The Sea Dragons held one another's paws tightly as they broke through the surface and up into the sunlight. They were bobbing between two palm-tree-covered islands.

Zoe had a brief chance to look around before the wave curled around her and the others again. Zoe clung to her friends with all her might.

"Get ready," Zoe warned Grace and Sofia. "I think we're about to go for another ride!"

6

The wave lifted high in the air. Then it surged

forward, carrying the three friends with it. Zoe

clung firmly to her friends and squeezed her

eyes shut. The wave kept spinning them one

way and then the other. Usually Zoe felt strong

in her Sea Dragon form. But this powerful wave

made her feel like she was riding the wildest roller coaster ever.

"Stay calm," Splashi said as she paddled furiously by her side.

Zoe knew Splashi was right. Surfing had taught her that in difficult situations, it was better to go with the wave than try to fight it. And anyway, Zoe was pretty sure this wave was taking them to land.

Sure enough, a moment later Zoe felt sand below her. Opening her eyes, she saw it was just as she had expected. The wave had dumped Zoe and her friends on the beach of the nearest island.

"That was exciting but really intense!" declared Grace, heaving herself up to sit on the sand.

"Totally," Sofia agreed, sitting beside Grace. "I can see why you enjoy surfing, Zoe. But I think I'll stick to diving."

"That was no normal wave. And you both did great," Zoe said. Zoe looked around for Splashi, to make sure she was okay. The tiny penguin was swimming away.

"See you soon!" she called, before diving into the water with barely a splash.

Zoe gazed about. "Just look at how amazing this island is! It's a great place to take a quick break."

"Yeah, we love it," said a nearby voice. "It's the perfect chill-out spot."

Zoe, Sofia, and Grace looked around. Farther up on the beach were some simple huts made from driftwood. Copper-colored seals leaned in the doorways, chatting to one another while fluffy seal cubs scampered around. Other sleepy-eyed seals stretched out on beach chairs made from palm leaves, sipping from coconut shells.

A seal waddled down the beach toward Zoe and her friends. He had impressive droopy whiskers and surprisingly curly tusks, like a ram's horns. Even more surprising were the three coconuts he had balanced in his flippers.

"Welcome to Seal Island," the seal said. "That was an awesome surf show you three put on. We couldn't have done it better ourselves."

Other seals came over, clapping their flippers enthusiastically.

"You three have totally earned a cool,

refreshing coconut juice," continued the seal with the tusks. "Here, catch!"

In one smooth movement, he dropped the coconuts onto his tail and flicked them at Zoe, Sofia, and Grace. The girls each caught one.

Zoe examined hers. She was very thirsty. But how was she going to get the juice out?

"Use a talon," Sofia suggested. She had already managed to open her coconut.

"That's what I did," Grace said, who had opened hers, too. She took a sip. "Wow! That's delicious!"

Zoe pressed a sharp talon to the top of the coconut. It easily pierced the tough shell. Zoe grinned. Being a dragon was so cool! She took a big gulp of juice. To her delight, her coconut tasted like mangoes and chocolate. Even better, it fizzed on her tongue. Right away, she felt her energy returning.

"Yo, look!" called one of the other seals, pointing a flipper out to sea. "There go some more waves, trying to break onto Big Wave Island."

The Sea Dragons turned to look. The other island was not far away. Like Seal Island, it was covered with palm trees and ringed with golden sand. But as they watched, something very odd happened. A wave rolled in to the island's beach, getting ready to break on the shore. But as it drew close, it hit what seemed to be an invisible barrier. As it touched the barrier, the wave turned to steam and evaporated. The same thing happened to the next wave, and then the next.

"That's so weird!" Grace cried.

"It is weird. And very uncool," said a big seal, his huge, liquid eyes sad. "Like, don't mess with the ocean, dude! The water is, like, super important. And no one can surf on steam."

Zoe felt her pulse begin to race.

"How long has this been going on?" she asked the seals.

"Well, I don't like to point the flipper at

anyone," said one of them, "but ever since the grumpy lady moved onto that island, things have been ... strange."

"Grumpy lady?" repeated Sofia.

"Yep, she moved onto Big Wave Island a couple of tides ago," the seal said. "She arrived on that same bizarro wave you guys came on. Except she seemed to be, like, controlling it."

"She gives off a negative energy," added another seal.

"Plus, she's got a hot temper. And I mean 'flames jumping out of her ears' hot. We offered her a welcome coconut. But she turned it to ash!"

"So rude, right? Like, who does that to a delicious welcome coconut?" said the big seal, shaking his head. "And ever since then, nothing has been able to get near the island. Neither animal nor wave. It's a real bummer because we used to surf there, like, all the time. Now there's this magical barrier around the island. You can't see it, but you sure can feel it when you get close. It's hot."

"The grumpy lady HAS to be the Fire Queen," Zoe said. "And the barrier protecting the island must be her doing."

Sofia and Grace nodded.

"But is that where the missing turtle is?" Grace wondered aloud.

That was exactly what Zoe wanted to know. "We need to check."

"But how?" Sofia asked. "You heard the seals. There's some sort of heat barrier all the way around the island."

Zoe turned to the seals. "You're locals. You know the waters around here better than anyone. Do you think there's any way to get onto that island?"

The seals exchanged a look. Zoe sensed they were trying to decide whether or not to tell her something. She got it. Surfers were often protective about their best surf spots.

"It's very important that we find a turtle that's gone missing," she told them softly. "She's one of the Sea Keepers. If we don't find her before the full moon, that grumpy lady might end up controlling—or even draining—the entire ocean."

That seemed to do the trick. The big seal nodded. "Clearly you three love the ocean as much as we do," he said. "There might be a way onto the island. But it won't be easy. How good are you at stunt surfing?"

7

"Stunt surfing?" repeated Zoe. "What's that?"

Once, she'd seen a surfing display where the

surfers rode on each other's shoulders. Was

this what the seals were talking about? She

couldn't see how riding on each other's shoul-

ders would help them get past the magical

barrier surrounding Big Wave Island!

"It will be easier if we show you," said one of the seals. "Grab a surfboard and follow us."

Zoe frowned, even more puzzled than before. Where were they going to get a surfboard?

The seal gestured behind them. There, sticking up out of the sand, was a row of surfboards. They were all decorated with swirly designs.

"Wow!" Grace said. "Did you make these?"

"We sure did," the seal said proudly. "We use driftwood that washes up on the shore. Now, who is ready to do some daredevil moves?"

Zoe looked at her friends. She could tell they were unsure about stunt surfing. She had been surfing for years and even she was nervous! "How about you guys sit this one out?" she suggested.

Sofia looked tempted but shook her head. "We can't make you do it alone."

"We're a team, remember?" Grace added.

Zoe's heart felt warm. It was so nice that her friends didn't want to let her down! But it was also clear they were still worn out from their last surfing adventure.

"You two can watch for danger from the shore," said Zoe, thinking fast. "That will make things way safer for me."

"Really? Okay!" said Sofia, looking reluctant and relieved at the same time.

"I guess that makes sense." Grace nodded. "Be careful!"

"I will," Zoe promised.

She flew over to the surfboards, trying to decide which one to choose. They all looked great! Finally, she picked one with a swirling wave painted on it. The wave was breaking onto sand that was the same color as her own dragon scales. It was perfect!

Zoe smiled. She had been feeling tired after their surf. But the moment she picked up the board, she felt energy surge through her. This always happened. Zoe's dad used to say she would keep surfing until she fell asleep on her board, if he let her.

"Come on, Sea Dragon," the seals called. They were already in the water, bobbing along on their boards. "Surf's up!"

"On my way!" Zoe called back.

Gripping her chosen board, Zoe flew down the beach toward the water. Even in the air, the board wanted to surf, twisting this way and that on gusts of wind. When she arrived at the water's edge, Zoe whooshed down, landing in the sea with a splash.

A group of seals joined her, paddling their boards expertly away from the shore.

"We need to paddle closer to the other island," explained a seal near Zoe who was on an orange board.

Zoe nodded, her excitement building. Being in the water was always great, in her opinion. And right now, she couldn't believe she was surfing with seals!

As the little group approached the neighboring island, the waves began to pick up. Zoe could now see the shimmering air of the heat barrier around the island. It looked like the air above a very hot pan or barbecue. She could also hear a sizzle as waves hit the barrier and turned to steam.

Her stomach did a little flip. "Where is that heat coming from?" she wondered aloud.

"The Fire Queen has cast a spell over it," said a voice.

Zoe turned to see Splashi paddling up beside her on a tiny purple board of her own!

"She wants to stop anyone from getting close to the island," Splashi explained. "The only way to break the spell is by stepping onto the island."

Zoe frowned. Any wave that came close to the barrier was turned to steam.

"But there's no way to get onto the island," she said. "Doesn't that barrier go all the way around?"

The seal on the orange board paddled over. "Ah! But we think there is a way," he said in his low, sleepy voice. "We've been watching. Quick, catch this wave and we'll show you."

Zoe felt the water swell beneath her. A wave was definitely forming. It was a big one, too. Her heart thumped. Was she ready to catch it?

"Of course you're ready," Splashi said, seeming to know Zoe's thoughts.

Zoe gripped her board tightly as the wave approached. Normally when she surfed, she jumped up onto her feet. But as a Sea Dragon, Zoe had to stay on her belly. *But the seals surf this way*, she told herself, *and so can I.*

The wave grew closer by the second. "What's the plan?" she asked the seals. "What sort of stunt do we have to do?"

"Just catch this wave," the nearest seal instructed. "Then we'll explain the stunt."

Zoe heard the wave drawing near with a familiar roar. She began to paddle hard, speeding up to match the wave's speed. Up and up the wave lifted. Zoe and the seals lifted, too, expertly moving their boards with the wave. Ahead, the heat barrier shimmered.

"We're getting close to that barrier," Zoe called out, a little nervously.

"Keep going," the seal on the orange board said calmly. "Let the wave lift you a bit higher."

"And then what?" asked Zoe. Did the seals actually have any idea what they were doing?

"Then you let go of the board," the seal explained, "and fly over the top of the barrier."

"Over the top? Are you sure the barrier doesn't go all the way around, like a dome?" Zoe called.

"We're pretty sure," the seal replied.

"Over the top? Well then, why can't I just fly in?" Zoe called.

"Because the gap is teeny-tiny," the seal said cheerfully. "The only way to be sure is to follow the water. But don't worry. We've seen birds fly through the gap. Most of them don't get scorched."

"MOST of them?" Zoe repeated.

She really wasn't sure that this was a good idea. Maybe she should drop out of this wave and go back to shore. But then Zoe noticed something. The shell on her bracelet was pulsing with light.

I'm going in the right direction, Zoe realized. Seeing the glow made her confident and determined. She was going to do this!

The heat barrier rose up before Zoe. It hissed like a snake. Clouds of steam billowed all around.

"Get ready to fly, Sea Dragon!" barked the

seals, each one turning just before they hit the barrier. "And watch out for that grumpy lady. She's on the island somewhere!"

"Remember, you can do this," Splashi called. "We can do this. Just follow the falling spray. Ready?"

Zoe nodded. Her ears were full of the sound of water and the hissing heat.

Beside her, faithful Splashi paddled furiously with her little flippers.

"One, two, three, FLY!"

8

Zoe crested the wave and let go of her board. Then, giving her wings a tremendous flap, she rose into the air. The heat barrier sizzled menacingly. As she approached the top of the wave, a sudden cloud of Fire Sparks appeared. They buzzed around Zoe's head, making her dizzy and jumbling her thoughts.

How am I supposed to get past the magical barrier again? she wondered. Was she supposed to fly under it somehow? Or push right through it? She couldn't remember!

Zoe shook her head, trying to clear her mind and get rid of the annoying sparks. Water droplets flung up into the air around her. Some hit the barrier and instantly turned to steam. But some of them did not! Instead, they arced up and over the top of the barrier. Then they began falling down through an invisible gap toward the island below.

"Follow the water!" Zoe roared with excitement, remembering what the seals had said.

Zoe flapped her wings again and surged

even higher. Following the path that the droplets had just taken, Zoe flew neatly over the
top of the heat barrier.

"Good work!" whooped Splashi, flying alongside Zoe. "Now we need to get onto the sand.
That's how the Fire Queen's spell will be
broken."

"Let's go, then!" Zoe said.

Zoe angled her body toward the island down below. She zoomed lower, feeling the air whoosh past. As the ground rushed up to meet them, Zoe stretched out her front paws, ready to steady herself. She slowed down, and a moment later her talons sank into the soft, warm sand.

Splashi did three midair somersaults. "You broke the spell!"

Had she? Zoe wanted to be sure. She launched herself back into the air and looked around from the higher vantage point. A wave was heading into shore. And this time, instead of turning to steam, it rolled in and broke on the sand . . . like a normal wave!

But Zoe had no time to enjoy her success. A swarm of Fire Sparks was back, and it was even bigger than before! The sparks were angrier, too. The hot little embers darted at Zoe and Splashi, stinging any part of them they could reach.

Zoe lashed at them with her tail and roared as loudly as she could. But the effort of all that surfing and flying had tired her out. She just couldn't roar loudly enough to keep the sparks away. Worse, her head was beginning to swirl again.

What am I doing on this island? If only she could just rest for a moment...

Suddenly, there came a massive roar. Surfing

onto shore were Grace and Sofia. Her friends had arrived! It was the most wonderful sight. Instantly, all Zoe's tiredness vanished.

"You came!" she cried.

"Of course we came!" Grace replied.

"We couldn't leave you to deal with the Fire Sparks on your own," Sofia added.

Grace and Sofia dove off their boards and into the water. Zoe grinned. She knew what her friends were doing. Like the last time they were in the Magic Forest, they were charging up their roars with seawater power!

The sight of the other Sea Dragons seemed to drive the Fire Sparks into a frenzy. They whirled around Zoe fiercely. But now that Zoe knew help was on the way, everything felt different. Her friends would help her deal with the sparks. Sure enough, when Grace and Sofia surged back out of the water, they roared out powerful misty clouds. Their sea roars wrapped around the buzzing Fire Sparks, putting them out instantly.

"Great work!" Zoe whooped, giving her friends midair wing-hugs.

"We started surfing over the moment we saw you get over the heat barrier," said Sofia.

"You made it disappear!" Grace said, her voice full of admiration. "How did you do that?"

"It was a magic spell," Zoe explained. "And the moment I touched the sand, the spell was broken."

Zoe felt so much better with her friends by her side. "Come on, let's go find that missing turtle."

"Where should we look?" Sofia wondered as the three Sea Dragons soared higher into the air.

"Good question," Grace said. "This island isn't very big, but it's covered with palm trees. It could take a long time to find a turtle hidden in them."

For a moment Zoe felt worried. Grace had a point. But then Zoe felt a tugging on her wrist.

Once again, the shell was glowing with aqua light.

"I think my bracelet is going to lead us," she said to her friends. "Come on, this way."

The bracelet guided Zoe over to the thick grove of trees in the island's center. Zoe flew lower, zigzagging through the palms. Her friends followed close behind. It was a beautiful island, but Zoe could sense that something was not quite right. The others clearly felt it as well.

"There are no birds singing," Grace observed. "It's like the whole island is holding its breath."

"I can hear something, though," Sofia said. "Listen. Hear that soft, crackling sound?"

Zoe could hear it. But what was it? When they rounded a bend, Zoe found out. They had reached a small clearing in the palm trees. On the sandy ground was a ring of fire. And in the middle of the fire was a huge turtle shell. The creature's legs and head were safely tucked inside.

Zoe's bracelet began to flash.

Zoe gasped. "The missing Sea Keeper! Quick! Let's get her out of there."

"I wouldn't try that if I were you," said a nasty voice.

Zoe turned. At first she thought she was looking at the sun. But when the bright glow moved, Zoe realized it was actually a fiery woman hovering in the air. She was dressed in fire, and her hair was long and flaming.

The Sea Dragons spoke as one. "The Fire Queen!"

9

The Fire Queen smiled evilly.

"I am so glad you are smart enough to recognize me. I must admit, I suspected you three weren't very bright. Do you truly believe you can stop me from carrying out my plan?"

"Do you mean your plan to keep this Sea Keeper prisoner and destroy the ocean?" Zoe retorted fiercely. "Because yes, we are definitely going to stop that!"

The Fire Queen's expression changed. "Then you are even more foolish than I thought," she snarled. "You will regret your meddling."

"Watch out!" Splashi squeaked, flapping her flippers in alarm.

The Fire Queen whirled in a circle. Fire Sparks rose from her hair and dress, buzzing and crackling as they flashed around. The air, which was already hot, became hotter still. Then suddenly, the sparks zoomed toward the Sea Dragons. Their glow was so bright that Zoe had to close her eyes. But she could still hear

them, sizzling as they flashed past. She could also feel them, stinging her dragon scales.

Zoe felt like she was lost in the middle of the ocean, uncertain which way to swim to reach the shore. That horrible dizziness and confusion was starting to overwhelm her.

"Roar power is the only way to deal with the sparks," Splashi said urgently.

Zoe knew that Splashi was right. But this was easier said than done. When Zoe opened her eyes, the Fire Sparks were everywhere. It was like the air was on fire. Through the blinding haze, Zoe could just make out Grace and Sofia. They batted at the sparks with their wings and talons.

But the sparks just wouldn't give up. Even worse, the Fire Queen whirled around them all, making more and more new sparks.

Zoe gritted her teeth. She was not going to let the Fire Queen win. "We need to roar," she called to Grace and Sofia.

Zoe could tell her friends were as dizzy and confused as she was. But they nodded all the same. Together, the Sea Dragons opened their mouths and roared. They tried their best, but the roars could barely be heard over the crackling of Fire Sparks.

The Fire Queen threw back her head and laughed, sending sparks spewing into the air. "Pathetic Sea Dragons! Why would anyone think water is more powerful than fire? It is clear: Water is no match for fire at all. Soon all this water will be gone and fire will rule!"

The Fire Queen pushed both hands toward the Sea Dragons, sending a wave of hot, magical air at them. The blast threw Zoe, Grace, and Sofia tumbling back. They somersaulted through the air and landed with an enormous splash in the water.

Zoe opened her eyes underwater. As a Sea Dragon, she could see just as clearly under the water as she could above it. The first thing she spotted was Splashi, swimming beside her.

"Don't give up, Zoe," she urged.

But there was no need for her little friend to say this. Zoe had no intention of giving up! In fact, the Fire Queen had made a big mistake sending them flying into the ocean. After all, this was where a Sea Dragon got her strength from! With the salt water all around her, Zoe felt her energy returning. Her mind was sharp again.

Grace and Sofia swam up next to Zoe.

"It was kind of the Fire Queen to give us a chance to recharge our roars, wasn't it?" Grace said, her eyes twinkling mischievously.

"Just what I was thinking!" Sofia agreed. "Should we go and say thanks?"

Zoe laughed, filling the water with bubbles as Splashi did encouraging loops nearby. Zoe grabbed hold of her friends' paws. They would show the Fire Queen that Sea Dragons never gave up.

"Let's go!" Zoe cried.

Together they burst out of the ocean, sending sprays of water flying. Energy pulsed through Zoe as she and her friends zoomed back to the Fire Queen. The fiery ring around the turtle burned even more brightly than before. The Fire Queen hovered nearby, keeping guard.

When she spotted the Sea Dragons, she cried out in anger and charged at them.

Zoe looked at her friends and nodded. No words were needed. Zoe felt the roar building inside her. She held it in as the Fire Queen drew closer.

"Haven't given up yet?" the Fire Queen growled. Her flaming hair whipped around her frowning face. "How would you like another blast of firepower?"

But the Sea Dragons were ready. Just as the Fire Queen launched another heat wave at them, Zoe, Grace, and Sofia roared. A shimmering seawater mist filled the air. It crashed into the queen's rippling heat wave, destroying it with a hiss of steam.

Yelling with fury, the Fire Queen whirled around and flew in the opposite direction.

"She's heading back to the turtle!" Zoe called to her friends. "Hurry! We've got to get there first."

The friends charged after the Fire Queen,

flying as fast as they could. The queen tried to slow them down by sending a gust of hot air over her shoulder at them. But Zoe simply jumped on and let the warm air carry her up over the Fire Queen!

"Thanks for the lift!" she called down to the Fire Queen.

"Stop right now!" screamed the furious queen, sending a fireball at Grace and Sofia.

But the Sea Dragons quickly extinguished the blazing mass with another seawater roar.

Zoe skidded down onto the sand, stopping just before the fire ring around the giant turtle shell. The flames were leaping high. Was the turtle okay inside that shell? And would Zoe have enough roar left in her to extinguish the blaze?

"You can do it, Zoe!" Splashi cheered, landing by her side.

Zoe took in a big breath. Roaring with all her might, she directed her dragon energy at the fiery ring trapping the turtle. The flames flickered and burned lower, but they did not go out completely.

"Leave my fire alone!" screeched the Fire Queen, hovering above.

But Zoe paid no attention. Neither did her friends. As Zoe roared once more, Grace and Sofia landed beside her to join in. Together, they roared their biggest roar yet! Finally, the

fiery ring around the turtle died away com-

pletely. A moment later, all that was left was a

puff of smoke.

10

Zoe looked up at the Fire Queen. Her muscles were tense and ready. Was the queen about to come down and continue the battle? But with one last angry howl, the furious queen flew off in a flash of fire. Her Fire Sparks followed in a bright, buzzing stream behind her.

"You did it!" Splashi cried, doing loops in the air.

Zoe's aches and tiredness vanished as she flew up to her friends, whooping with delight. "Sea Dragons win again!" she cheered. "Tail slap!"

Laughing, the three Sea Dragons flipped up their tails, slapping them together in a type of high five.

"Is it safe to come out now?" asked a muffled voice.

Down on the ground, the turtle's head peeked out from its beautiful polished shell.

"Totally safe," Sofia assured the turtle.

The turtle's head and flippers popped out from the shell. She looked around.

"Would you like us to give you a ride back into the sea?" Grace asked.

"No need for that," the turtle said. "You've already done enough by rescuing me!"

Then she headed straight for the water.

"Wow, that's the fastest turtle I've ever seen!" Sofia said.

"Well, we'd probably be the same if anyone tried to keep us out of the water for long!" Grace laughed.

When the turtle reached the shoreline, she splashed joyfully into the waves.

Zoe cocked her head. "Can you hear that? It sounds kind of flappy. And ... squeaky?"

The Sea Dragons looked at one another, puzzled.

Then Sofia burst out laughing. "I bet I know what that noise is." She scanned the water. "Look!"

Heading to shore on the crest of a wave were the hatchling turtles! They had spotted their leader and were swimming toward her as fast as they could. Their little fins flapped furiously and they squeaked with happiness.

"You're okay!" they squealed, climbing onto the huge turtle's back to catch their breath.

"And look how far we came! We swam all this way by ourselves! Are you hurt?"

"I am fine, thanks to these dragons," the Sea Keeper said, pointing her flipper up at the Sea Dragons hovering in the sky above. "They were very brave to fight the Fire Queen and her sparks."

"But we were brave, too, weren't we?" the hatchlings asked. "We had to swim a very long way to get here."

"So brave," the big turtle said tenderly. "And now, it's time to head home." She looked up at the Sea Dragons. "Would you like to come to Turtle Town?" she asked. "You would be most welcome. We will throw a feast for you in our town hall. Our turtle chefs make a delicious seagrass-and-algae curry."

Zoe gulped. She did not like the sound of that at all! Then she noticed something. The shell on her bracelet was glowing. Looking over at her friends, she saw that Grace's and Sofia's shells were also glowing.

"I'm so sorry," she said politely to the Sea Keeper. "We must return home ourselves."

The turtle nodded her wise old head understandingly. "Going on adventures is wonderful. But going home is the best part. Goodbye, brave Sea Dragons. And thanks again!"

With that, the big turtle dove down under the waves.

"Wait for us!" cried the hatchlings who weren't already riding on the big turtle's back.

A moment later, all the turtles had disappeared below the surface.

Zoe's bracelet glowed brighter than ever. She could feel it tugging her, ever so gently, toward Grace's and Sofia's shells.

"The shells want to join up," Zoe said, slipping

the bracelet off and holding it in her paws. "Like last time."

Sure enough, when Grace and Sofia held their shells next to Zoe's, the three shells clicked together. There was a bright flash of light. When it faded, the three shells had become one.

Zoe leaned over it eagerly. The surface of the large shell flickered and the Tree Queen's face appeared, smiling broadly.

"Congratulations, Sea Dragons!" she said, her warm, rich voice vibrating out of the shell. "Once again, you have succeeded in your quest. Thanks to you, two of the three Sea Keepers are now free!"

Zoe felt a warmth spread through her. It had definitely been a challenging quest. Surfing on a wave crested with fire was no easy feat. Fighting the foggy feelings from the Fire Sparks had made it even more difficult. But Zoe had also loved it. Being in the water with her friends was just about the best thing in the world, after all.

"You'll need us back, won't you?" Zoe asked.

"Yes," said the Tree Queen. "There is still one missing Sea Keeper. The Fire Queen has not given up. I suspect she is going to make things even more fiery next time. And it is drawing closer to the time when the Water Watch must be wound. If that doesn't happen by the next full moon, the seas of the Magic Forest will be in jeopardy. Tell me, Sea Dragons—are you prepared to help us again?"

Zoe, Grace, and Sofia did not need to look at one another. The answer burst out of them all at the same time. "Yes!"

The Tree Queen swayed her branches in a pleased way. "Then I will see you three again soon. Until next time, Sea Dragons. And now, I will guide each of you back home."

The image faded from the shell.

Zoe remembered how last time they had been in the Magic Forest, the shells had split apart after the queen had finished speaking to them. So Zoe gave the shell a gentle tug, and the large shell instantly split into three perfect parts again.

Zoe turned to Grace and Sofia, and the three friends hugged. "See you soon!" said Zoe.

It was hard to leave this magical wonder-land. But knowing she was going back to camp definitely made it easier.

Zoe flew a little way off and held her shell to her ear. Mixed in with the sound of the waves came the voice of the Tree Queen.

"Catch the next wave, Zoe!"

Looking out, Zoe saw a wave starting to form on the horizon. Zoe did not need to be asked twice to catch a wave! She slid her bracelet back around her wrist and whooshed lower to greet the wave. Her tail skimmed along the water's surface as the wave curled over her. Faster and faster she went, through the sparkling tube of water, until finally the wave collapsed down over her.

Zoe plunged into the sea, feeling the water bubbling around her. Then, as the water cleared, she swam to the surface and back into the air.

Amazingly, Zoe's yellow surfboard was right there, bobbing on the water!

"Nice surfing!" called a voice. Stef, the surfing coach, was paddling toward her on her own board, a huge smile on her face. "You rode that monster wave for ages! But it's time to head in now. Have you had a good day?"

"The best!" Zoe grinned, climbing onto her board to paddle back to shore with Stef. "And I can't wait to do it all again really soon!"

Turn the page for a special sneak

peek of Sofia's adventure!

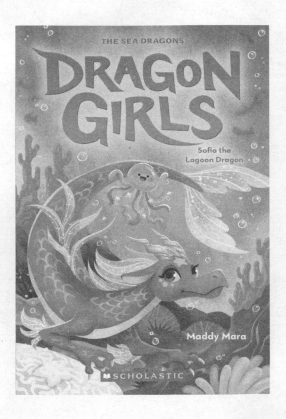

1

The last day of aquatics camp was here. They were celebrating by having a party at the nearby lagoon. Sofia curled her toes around the edge of the rock and looked around.

From the moment they arrived, Sofia could tell the lagoon was a special place. The water was surrounded by rocky cliffs and lush greenery. It glittered like a precious jewel. There was an impressive waterfall that flowed over the rocks before tumbling into the lagoon. The camp counselors had decorated the tall palm trees with paper lanterns, making everything look truly magical. Best of all, to one side was a long table, loaded with tasty things to eat and drink.

"Sofia! Coming for a swim before we eat?"

Sofia looked over. On the little beach were her cabinmates and new besties, Grace and Zoe. They waved at her. Sofia smiled and waved back.

Normally, it took her a little while to make

friends. But she had clicked instantly with Grace and Zoe. Maybe it was because they all loved water. Or maybe it was because they shared an amazing secret. The three girls had the ability to travel to a place called the Magic Forest. This was a beautiful land, ruled by the kindly Tree Queen. In the Magic Forest, Sofia and her friends were no longer normal girls. They became Sea Dragons! As Sea Dragons, they had powerful mermaid-like tails that helped them swim very fast underwater. They also had strong wings so they could fly high above the treetops.

Sofia loved how she could roar as a dragon.

For a start, roaring was fun. But it was more than that. The Sea Dragons' roars had amazing magical powers!

But the Magic Forest was facing a terrible threat. There was an evil Fire Queen who was trying to destroy the seas surrounding the forest. She had kidnapped three Sea Keepers, who were in charge of looking after the seas and keeping them in balance.

So far, Sofia, Grace, and Zoe had rescued two of the missing Sea Keepers: the dolphin leader and the sea turtle. Sofia couldn't wait to return and help rescue the third and final one.

"I'll be there in a sec," Sofia called to her friends. "I just want to do one dive."

Sofia loved diving. She had come to camp so she could work on her diving skills. She had learned a lot during the daily training sessions at the camp's dive pool. Just today, she had perfected her reverse dive. It had been so cool! She really wanted to try it out again.

The late-afternoon light was slowly turning the water from bright blue to purple. Low on the horizon, a full moon was rising. Sofia shivered with happiness. This was the perfect setting for a dive! Once again, she looked down. She had already checked with her dive instructor, Mel, that the lagoon was safe, and deep enough for diving. The water was so clear, she could see all the way down. The bottom of the lagoon was strewn with smooth pebbles that glimmered like treasure.

I'll dive down there and scoop one up, Sofia decided.

As she prepared herself to dive, she heard something. It was a song. At first Sofia thought one of the kids down below was singing. Or perhaps the counselors were playing music?

Magic Forest, Magic Forest, come explore . . .

Then Sofia smiled. She had heard this song twice before and knew what it meant. She was going to return to the Magic Forest! She looked at the bracelet on her wrist. On the silver chain hung a white, fan-shaped shell. The Tree Queen had given it to her the first time she and her friends had visited the Magic Forest. Grace and Zoe had bracelets just like it.

Right now, Sofia's shell was glowing pale pink. Excitement bubbled inside her, but she kept her breath steady and her mind focused. She ran through the steps of the dive in her head, making sure she had them straight. As she did so, she heard the song, louder than before.

Magic Forest, Magic Forest, come explore.

"*Don't worry, Magic Forest. I'm coming!*" Sofia murmured.

Then, with a last steadying breath, she jumped up into the air. The colors of the lagoon swirled by in a blur as she somersaulted backward. Sofia plunged into the lagoon's glassy surface. Cool water rushed past her as she dove down to the lagoon bed. As she plunged, the water seemed to change. It felt softer somehow. Then, as Sofia reached out for a gleaming stone, she heard the last line of the song.

Magic Forest, Magic Forest, hear my roar!

Grabbing the stone, Sofia began swimming back to the surface. Above her, through the water, Sofia could see the wonky outline of the full moon. It had a shimmery, silvery-pink glow to it. Sofia kicked hard, swimming up with all her might.

Bursting through the surface, she took a big gulp of air and looked around. A huge smile crept over her face. For just as she had expected, everything had changed!

ABOUT THE AUTHORS

Maddy Mara is the pen name of Australian creative duo Hilary Rogers and Meredith Badger. Hilary and Meredith have been making children's books together for many years. They love dreaming up new ideas and always have lots of projects bubbling away. When not writing, Hilary can be found cooking weird things or going on long walks, often with Meredith. And Meredith can be found teaching English online all around the world or daydreaming about being able to fly. They both currently live in Melbourne, Australia. Their website is maddymara.com.

DRAGON GAMES

PLAY THE GAME. SAVE THE REALM.

READ ALL OF TEAM DRAGON'S ADVENTURES!

DRAGON GIRLS

THE GLITTER DRAGONS

DRAGON GIRLS

Azmina the Gold
Glitter Dragon

Maddy Mara

THE GLITTER DRAGONS

DRAGON GIRLS

Willa the Silver
Glitter Dragon

Maddy Mara

THE GLITTER DRAGONS

DRAGON GIRLS

Naomi the Rainbow
Glitter Dragon

Maddy Mara

THE TREASURE DRAGONS

DRAGON GIRLS

Mei the Ruby
Treasure Dragon

Maddy Mara

THE TREASURE DRAGONS

DRAGON GIRLS

Aisha the Sapphire
Treasure Dragon

Maddy Mara

THE TREASURE DRAGONS

DRAGON GIRLS

Quinn the Jade
Treasure Dragon

Maddy Mara

THE NIGHT DRAGONS

DRAGON GIRLS

Rosie the
Twilight Dragon

Maddy Mara

THE NIGHT DRAGONS

DRAGON GIRLS

Phoebe the
Moonlight Dragon

Maddy Mara

THE NIGHT DRAGONS

DRAGON GIRLS

Stella the
Starlight Dragon

Maddy Mara

Collect them all!